That Which Makes Us Who We Are

Alex Mitchell

Published by Alex Mitchell, 2023.

THAT WHICH MAKES US WHO WE ARE

First edition. October 13, 2023.

Copyright © 2023 Alex Mitchell.

ISBN: 979-8891980129

Written by Alex Mitchell.

Also by Alex Mitchell

Chapter 1

The regal bone structure of the Congress Hotel flaunted the Majestic Grandeur of the aged facility. She stood 28 stories tall and was the product of countless renovations and fittings. The main lobby had a large open area with grey marble tile. The tile led to the check-in desk. From this view, you could see a water fountain in the lobby.

The rooms from the main structure were of atrium configuration. Guest rooms from the second floor to the 28th circled the atrium, and a large hollow area led upward to a stained-glass roof. A red rod iron railing on all the floors surrounding the atrium kept anything or anyone from being pushed or dropped off the center and descending onto the lobby's center.

Ramona and Lizzy stood reconciling the receipts.

The reconciliation in a hotel is done in the middle of the night. All the cash registers from all over the Hotel are balanced to account for every penny taken in. Gift shops, bars, and restaurants must match the revenue collected.

"No matter how much of that nasty coffee you pour me, I aint waking up any faster," Lizzy remarked to Ramona as Ramona poured more coffee into Lizzy's cup. Both women were young recent graduates from a hotel-motel management program. Ramona was an unremarkable-looking black girl aspiring to climb the corporate ladder oozing from every pore.

Lizzy was a plain-looking redhead girl with a pale complexion and glass that looked three sizes too large for her face.

"Why do they give access to cash registers to so many people that just can't count?" Lizzy commented.

"I wish they were stealing. At least we could have them fired." Ramona remarked.

"I think it's in the Constitution that you cannot fire someone for being stupid."

Suddenly a loud crash and splashing sound came from the direction of the lobby. Ramona and Lizzy sat briefly in the small office behind the reservation desk staring wide-eyed at each other.

"Oh God, what was that?" Lizzy was first to exclaim though the sentiment was mutual.

"We go look together." Ramona rationalized.

The women creep too slowly with their arms interlocked to the desk. There in the center of the hotel fountain was the source of the loud noise. A buxom blonde girl lye wearing only a baby doll nighty top, and Her head was wrenched into a contorted position, showing she was dead.

Her crystal blue eyes stared out toward Ramona and Lizzy. Whatever this woman's eyes wanted to convey was now eternally lost to this world. The dyed blue water from the fountain continued to pump, and slowly, the blue of the water became red and overflowed onto the lobby floor.

Ramona and Lizzy heard a stirring and muffled conversation. They looked up. On the 9th floor, at the railing, was a circle of faces of guests in various stages of shock and disbelief. When the guest saw that Ramona and Lizzy noticed them, the faces disappeared, and the unmissable rustle of mass packing began.

"We had better call the cops." Lizzy offered.

"Bullshit, we had better call the resident. He can call the cops."

"Mr. Wakefield, maybe you can explain the laps between when your staff discovered the body and when it was reported."

Detective Blake asked. In many hotels, there is a resident manager. This manager usually lives on the hotel property and is responsible when things happen at odd hours.

Detective Blake, an athlete-looking man in his mid-thirties, had convinced the small group into the office behind the reservations desk. The group consisted of Ramona and Lizzy, as well as Detective Yolanda Carter, Detective Blakes's partner, and two uniformed officers that had been the first to respond to the call. Hiram Wakefield was a thin-paste complexion man with an oversized Adam's apple protruding from his throat. Mr. Wakefield appeared still in shock over the discovery. He sweated profusely and consumed more than his share of the small room oxygen.

"Look, I have contacted the legal rep for the Hotel, and he should be here shortly. Until he arrives, I don't think it would be wise to answer any questions."

Wakefield offered in a shaky voice.

"Look, dick face; no one is trying to get you to confess. We have some general questions to help us categorize the event." Detective Carter noted, eyeing the group. Carter's stare rested on Ramona, and Ramona defiantly returned the gaze. "Let's do an easy question, what are the dead girls' names?'

"How would I know?" Wakefield answered.

"Don't you get the names of your guest?" Blake asked.

"I never said she is or was a guest."

"Oh, Hiram, please don't try to tell me some blonde double D wanders in off the street and walks up to the front desk and says, excuse me, I seem to have lost my underpants. Can you help me find them?"

At this point, the uniformed officers, who had been virtually unnoticed, began chucking at Detective Carter's actions.

"Nine. She came from the ninth floor." Ramona answered.

Hiram Wakefield pointed a long bony finger at Ramona.

"You could be fired for giving out information on a guest."

"Sir, if you fire her for cooperating with an authorized official, she can sue the Hotel. The Hotel would have no choice but to sue you for mismanagement and misrepresentation." Blake informed Wakefield.

"That's right, Hiram baby, she could have you sued out of your jockey shorts. Not that you will need them because if you keep obstructing an active investigation, you could end up in jail playing every night is date night with the brothers in a small romantic prison cell." Carter gave Wakefield a wink that seemed to dissolve the last of his resolves.

"Sounds like it's time to round up everyone on the ninth floor for some questions," Blake announced to one of the uniformed officers.

"You can't," Lizzy said in a small voice. She had been almost totally hidden behind Ramona.

"And why the hell not?" Carter asked in a loud voice.

"Because they all checked out," Lizzy answered.

Blake and Carter turned and stared at Wakefield, totally speechless.

"Cuff this son of a bitch and read him his rights."

These where the first words Carter was able to form.

Chapter 2

"When did it all change? And why did it all change." Robert Bobby Bond asked himself.

It seemed like yesterday; he was in the military fighting for the American way. And it also seemed like just yesterday he had strapped on his first police badge, swearing to protect and serve. Now even the meeting places and offices have changed. He had been called to a meeting in the Met Square Building in Downtown St. Louis, A 42-floor office building that housed countless businesses. Nothing like meeting in the old Deer Street Police Station, he thought. The people were different. So many of them made him feel uncomfortable. His cop instincts shouted at him to notice things around him that did not bother anyone.

He noticed a young Asian woman on his way in, but there was no particular reason for her to seem out of place to him.

A pair of Black teenage male twins seemed to look down as he entered the doorway. But maybe they wondered if he was one of the cops from a cop incident they had watched on the news. Could it be that the very cop instincts he had spent his life honing and had saved his ass countless times were now turning against him? He could remember when he thought of a person of sixty as a relic—a fossil.

Too old to have any value in life, just skin and bone waiting to deteriorate and blow away as dust. Now here he was, Sixty-six, and somehow, good health and a strong body had played the cruelest pranks on him.

The room was full of people in small groups clustered together, babbling in various forms of shorthand English. Some women seemed hell-bent on looking like men, and men looked eager to hide any lingering traces of masculinity.

Bobby knew he wasn't a homophobic person. He was an I don't care about your sexual orientation person. So why do you want to try to make me a part of something I don't care about type of person? Keep your crap to yourself; he remembered a drill sergeant telling him, or maybe it was a watch commander. It all seemed to meld at some point, not that it made any difference.

Bobby noticed an information sign over a booth in the middle of the lobby and decided to approach a young black woman behind the counter. The black woman was filing her fingernails, which were too long to perform any practical task.

"Winters and Slay?" Bobby asked, and the woman paused, filing her nails just long enough to give him a look design to express her dissatisfaction at being interrupted in a critical part of the nail filing process. She blinked her large, overly made-up eyes at him, then pointed toward a directory on the wall next to a set of elevators.

"Sorry to have bothered you," Bobby stated in wasted sarcasm.

"Ten." A slender young woman in a neat pants suit instructed Bobby as he raced to enter the elevator just before it closed. She turned her back to him to secure the illusion of privacy as she continued a cell phone call now that she had discharged his duty to ensure a floor for her. She was, however, unaware that he had already selected Ten as it was the floor he was looking for as well.

"Look, I'm a big girl. I know what I signed up for. It's just that this is not the way to let it go." She muttered into the telephone. Even though Bobby could not hear the other side of the conversation, it was clear from her breathing pattern that she was not taking the news she was being given well. It was an

I *will* always care about your call, The call where the person on the other end didn't even have the dignity to dump someone in person call.

Bobby sprang free to enjoy the freedom from the confinement of the elevator and another person's misery. There in front of him was a familiar face, at least.

"Betty." Bobby bellowed almost too loud. An old friend from his cop days on the north side of St. Louis. A link to the past. A reassurance that he was in the right world. Betty rushed to Bobby and hugged him with the vitality of a woman half her age. But there, the similarities ended. When he hugged her, he no longer felt the firm vibrant, sexy woman he had known fifteen-plus years ago but a Spector of her. As she hugged him, he could feel her bones beneath her flesh and dress like handling a cat. The breast he had once fantasized about mushed in as though the front of her was some form of foam replacement. But her eyes and smile were still there, glowing like a lighthouse beacon welcoming an old friend's home.

"I am so glad someone was able to talk you out of complete retirement." Betty smiled, and light seemed to flow through her.

"I heard Sam needed someone to ride shotgun on a couple of cases."

Betty gave Bobby a quizzical look and started to say something, then chose something different. "Cornel Morrison is waiting for you inside. I think there is quite a bit he needs to tell you himself."

Betty pointed toward the main office doors. "I am training a new assistant this morning. Why don't I arrange to bring you coffee."

Bobby was caught in what he often thought of as cops' confusion. He knew something was missing from the conversation but had no idea what it was.

Furthermore, he had no idea if whatever was missing was important. He walked to the door and steadied himself. The room may be full of men his age on respirators having a meeting using stomas.

"Get your ass in here, Bond." Cornel Jack Ironman Morrison bellowed as Bobby timidly opened the office door. Morrison was a retired Navy Seal and head of investigations for Winters and Slay.

Morrison was a thick-neck man that looked like a college football coach. Bobby had huge biceps and a broad chest, but Morrison looked just as strong even though he was five years older.

Bobby heard someone enter the room behind him and turned to see the young woman from the elevator. She had gone to the lady's room to recover from the emotional conversation.

"One cream. Two sugars." Bobby assumed this must be the assistant in training.

She stared at Bobby.

"One cream. Two sugars."

Morrison had a stern face that looked like a smile might crack it, but at the looks between the woman and Bobby, Morrison could not help being risk the smile. "Bond, this is not the receptionist but your new partner."

"The fuck you say, Sir," Bobby yelled.

"Robert Bobby Bond meets Sam Boone." Morrison introduced.

"With all due respect, I worked for fifteen years with Sam Boone, and that aint him. Hell, as far as I can tell, that aint even him."

"Thank you for the compliment, Pops," Sam responded.

"Look, kid; you might want to watch your mouth."

"Sorry. I meant to say Grand Pa."

"It's good to see you two are going to get along." Morrison started.

"Sir, who is this?"

"I am Sam Boone. Do you want to see my driver's license?"

"Yes, and then show me your Johnson rod. No manner of reassignment surgery on this planet could turn my old partner into a hot young girl." Bobby was now in rant mode.

"Hot. Really." Sam commented.

"How is that hot? All you can take away from all this bellowing, young lady," Betty commented, entering the room with a young girl pushing a coffee service on a rolling cart. "This is Samantha Boone, your ex-partner's niece. She has been working here briefly, but she is quite good."

"I don't babysit." Bobby declared.

"I told you I don't need help. I can handle this on my own." Sam stated, giving Bobby a venomous once over.

"I call the shots. It's both of you, or it is no deal. I got a cold feeling in my gut that something is wrong with what we have been asked to do. I need the skill sets from both of you."

Bobby and Sam stood staring at each other now with the same problem. One that Morrison had caused. He had not outlined the job, and curiosity was starting to rage.

"Yeah, so what's the job?" Bobby finally asked.

Morrison looked at Samantha. "You in, or are you leaving the room?"

"I'm in, Sir. But if he tries to make me eat my vegetables, I might bite his arm off."

"Fair enough." Morrisons motioned for Sam and Bobby to be seated. Betty put two huge folders in front of the investigators. "We have been asked to escort a group of average citizens to depositions in various judge's chambers."

'Why are they being deposed?" Sam asked.

"I am told the is privileged and classified at this time." Morrisons answered.

Bobby raised his hand like a kid in class. "Don't the US Marshals or Sheriff's office handle this stuff?"

"That's the first knot in my colon. Yes, and they don't charge. The law firm is being paid top dollar for the service."

"You mean they are paying top dollar to keep everyone, including us, in the dark?" Bobby's comment seemed to give Sam a shiver.

"That's why you would not send a private investigator alone. There is something out there, and we don't know what." Sam assessed.

Chapter 3

"It's not like we are spies, George." Kia scolded George Kramer as he entered the coffee shop. Kia, Shannon, George, and David had agreed to meet in the last booth of a rundown coffee shop off Highway 109. Despite Kia's protest, they were all aware of the visit's clandestine nature. Kia Chung was an attractive girl of Korean descent in her mid-twenties. She worked in the accounting department for Sheffield Processing.

"We are all aware of your heroic spirit and acrobatic dexterity, Kia, but this shit scares me."

David Donaldson, a marketing specialist for Sheffield, led out.

"Last time I checked, you seemed to enjoy my athletic dexterity and flexibility, so don't be such a chicken."

"I agree with David; we are breaking the rules by meeting here to discuss the game. We all have spouses who would freak out if they had the slightest idea about what we are all involved in." Shannon, a young black girl with a light complexion and fluffy natural hair, began before being cut off by David.

"Look, I keep watching the news and checking the papers, and there is nothing. Not a word.

A girl ends up dead in a fountain in the middle of a four-star hotel. Naked to the world, and someone has the power to shut down every single word."

"It's the Game Masters doing." George wined. "We all are being subpoenaed to testify in a judge's chambers in a closed session, and no one wants to tell us what they are going to ask."

"Look, the game is the hottest thing on this planet, so it would stand to reason someone with juice is pulling the strings.

They will find out if Tracy's fall was an accident." Shannon stopped abruptly and stared at the eyeballs waiting for her next comment.

"Or if we have a killer among us."

"If we are voting. I vote we wait for contact from the Game Master. He has handled everything to this point, and anything we do, like going to the police, could undo whatever he has set up to fix the problem." David confidently offered.

"Who do you fix a dead girl, David." George snapped almost too loud and got a stare from the rest of the group.

"I liked her. I had sex with her on several occasions, but if she took her own life, there is no reason I know of for all of us to ruin our lives. Not to mention freaking out our spouses and families." David rationalized.

"Sorry, George, but I got to agree with David. It's too soon with too little information to pull the self-destruct switch." Kai remarked.

"Amen." Shannon chimed in.

Chapter 4

C hicago "Detectives Blake and Carter, please come in." The request came from Captain Marshal. Captain Marshal's request had little to do with a normal request. He ruled the detective squad with an iron hand. Blake and Carter had been summoned to his office but were unsure what to expect, nor did they feel they had enough information to speculate.

"I understand the two of you are in charge of investigating the woman found in the lobby fountain of the Congress Hotel.

"Yes, sir." Carter attempted to confirm.

"Don't interrupt. At this time, you will cease and desist all investigations into that incident. Any information you have collected thus far needs copies on my desk by today's end of the business day. You will not discuss this matter with anyone. Am I clear?"

"May we at least ask why?" Blake asked.

"Because that is a direct order from your commanding officer. You will comply or plan different forms of employment."

Speechless, Blake and Carter looked at each other.

They had barely begun an

investigation, and now it was being ripped from them and reassigned.

"Why are the two of you still in my office?"

Marshal yelled.

It did not take words for Blake and Carter to know they had stumbled into something that needed the lid shut on and fast.

"RISE AND SHINE." BOBBY sang out as Sam opened her apartment door. He had been knocking with the loud cop knock that made everyone aware someone was trying to get your attention. Sam opened the door and led Bobby in. She wore an oversized tee shirt, but her athletic frame was still noticeable. Her brunette hair was a mess, as was her apartment.

"I came bearing a peace offering." Bobby dumped the box he was carrying on her already-filled sofa.

"What's that?"

"A Kevlar vest. It should fit you. And a backup weapon."

"Are we invading a small country? I thought this was simple escort detail." Sam went into the tiny bathroom to start getting ready but left the door open so they could hear each other.

"Yesterday, when we left the office downtown, did you notice two black teenage boys that looked like twins?" Bobby asked.

"Yeah, the two with the dreadlocks; why?"

"They were following us."

Sam stuck her upper body out of the bathroom and was clearly naked from the waist up.

"Kid, please." Bobby gestured to shoe her back into the bathroom though he still could see her.

"Yeah, they were not only following us but showed up in the building before we got there."

"So, you are saying someone told them to be on the lookout for us, and we have been made."

"Made. Exactly. You talk cop. So here is the big twist. There was a small Asian woman outside the building, and when she saw them, she took their picture with her cell camera."

"Sounds like a lot of people know what is going on, just not us." Sam tried on the vest and found it fit perfectly. The spare weapon he brought was a Glock 19 9mm. "This is a lot better than my service weapon."

"Keep it. I have plenty, and I want to apologize for the Johnson Rod comment that was out of line."

"No need you had every right to be surprised. I thought someone had explained it to you."

"You thought I would stand there and insult you knowing who you were? Hey kid, I may be a caveman, but I aint that cruel."

A slight laugh passed between the two of them.

The little laugh did wonders for changing the mood between them.

"So, what do you say we go pick up that first person from the list? This time we will take my caddy. I get a cramp thinking about that Fiat you drive."

The first house of the client to be escorted lived in a South St. Louis neighborhood that was immaculate. All the houses were neat and extremely well-maintained.

The houses were large cottage-style made of brick. The places mainly looked the same, with small, customized additions to most. There were four-foot cyclone fences around the rear and side of the house, designed to keep pets from investigating the streets and the neighbor's trash. As Boddy and Sam walked to the house's front door, Bobby hesitated slightly. He couldn't see what it was, but there was something wrong. Bobby noticed the neighbor's dogs barking, but he had no way to see what the dog was barking at.

"My name is Lester Cooper; my wife is getting ready to go to the judge's office." A rail-thin man in a city services uniform informed them as he let them into the house. Lester looked back to be sure his wife could not hear his questions to Bobby and Sam.

"What is this all about? I mean, ten years of marriage, and now suddenly there are matters a wife can't discuss with her husband." Lester reeked of frustration.

"We don't know. No one will tell us either."
Bobby whispered.

"What did that company she works for do?"

"I thought you said you trust me, Lester."

The woman, Julie Cooper, the client to be escorted, appeared after hearing Lester's question.

There was a young girl, about 9 or 10 with Julie that looked like an earlier version of her, most likely her daughter accompanying Julie.

As Sam, Julie, and Bobby exited the house, the dog that had been barking began having a fit. Suddenly one of the dreadlock twins stood up from behind a rolling trash can and aimed a pistol at Julie. Sam hit Julie with a shoulder block, knocking Julie it the grasp of Bobby.

Sam drew her weapon and aimed for the teen but missed because Bobby had grabbed her by the collar and pulled her toward him. Bobby's experience told him to be watchful of the second twin. A second shot whizzed past Sam's head. It was the second of the twins firing from a better angle.

"Woman, what kind of filth have you tracked into our lives?" Was the only thing Lester was able to say as he hugged their daughter. The dreadlock twins took off with Olympic track record speed vaulting over four-foot fences like it was a game.

Even though Bobby and Sam made it to the judge's chambers late, they were allowed to have Julie enter her deposition. The judge had previously worked with Bobby and knew of his professionalism in the courts. The police had held Bobby and Sam on the crime scene longer than they would have liked. The same questions were asked over and over. But St. Louis City and County detectives work together frequently, and a degree of respect was afforded Bobby.

The police also stated that after her deposition, whatever it was, she would most likely be safe, but they would patrol as much as possible. Then added that this close to a high school, they could find sixty to seventy kids that matched the general description of the suspects in less than ten minutes.

"WHAT IS THIS SUPPOSED to be?" Bobby asked, examining the contents of a flat box that had been delivered to Sam's apartment. Bobby and Sam had tried to contact Cornel Morrison, but he was in conference.

"It's a vegan pizza with a cauliflower dough crust. It's good for you."

"That's your first mistake. Pizza is not supposed to be good for you.'

Sam chucked while seated on the floor, examining information on her laptop and flipping through the pages of the information she had received regarding their work. Bobby had chosen to clean and declutter her apartment to reach a deep thought process.

"Damn." She spoke.

"What's that? Did you find anything important?"

"If you mean other than the fact that I don't know if I feel comfortable with you bagging my trash and washing my dishes. I first thought this was some form of industrial accident cover-up."

"Oddly enough, my first thought too. No one wants the shareholders to know the reason the yearend bonus is small is that they paid some poor guy off who lost all his fingers in a Brown and Sharp turret lathe."

Sam smiled at Bobby's assessment as he sat on the sofa he had cleared. "Two problems with that theory. One company that seems to be involved is Sheffield Process in Earth City, Missouri, and Richmond Material Processing in Iowa."

"So, no matter how many of your fingers you cut off in Earth City, no one in Iowa will hear you scream. And by the way, where is the box this pizza came in? It has to taste better than this crappy pizza."

"Last comment excluded; you really are smarter than you look." Sam paused. "But how could you not be? I pulled up the online prospectus for both companies. No one on the deposition schedules is from the manufacturing floor."

"Could one company have supplied faulty equipment to the other?"

"Great guess? But wrong. I checked seems Richmond supplies raw materials, not machines." Sam grabbed a slice of the pizza and ate it like it was the best meal she had ever experienced. "Now, a question for you. What's up with you and Betty? And don't deny it; I saw how long she held that friendly welcome-back hug."

Bobby collected his thoughts for a moment and then put the pizza slice down. "We were friends in the past. She introduced me to Michelle—my late wife.

Back in the day, Betty was quite a matchmaker." Bobby stared into space as if watching a line of ghost dance from the room.

Sam produced a glass of wine for herself and a whiskey for Bobby. "Hardly seems fair. The matchmaker ends up the lonely old cat lady on the block."

"Is that why you were dating that married guy?" Bobby asked.

Sam thought for a moment, "On the elevator, you heard me breaking up with him. Nothing like a little eavesdropping." A coldness harbored in her tone.

"There is a new thing called cell phones. No one feels the need to have a private conversation in private anymore. Eavesdropping is a lost art form. And for the record, you didn't break up with him. He broke up with you." Bobby knocked back the remainder of the whiskey in the rock glass. Sam started to return the volley of comments, but they froze in her throat, and she turned her face away from Bobby. "Look, kid, he set you up. I was in a dentist's office, and they have only women's magazines, and I was reading this article."

Sam turned toward Bobby, now wondering where he was going. "The article said that men communicate for content and women communicate for frequency."

"What does that mean?" Sam refilled their glasses now, knowing he was not deliberately trying to hurt her feelings.

"Well, when a guy and a girl first start dating, they are in constant contact. Calls and emails, and texts. Conversely, you are career orientated, so this guy knew you would not be contacting him frequently and at all hours."

A look of recognition began to overtake Sam's face.

"He probably told you he and his wife were considering a divorce, and they led separate lives. That's where you living alone comes into play. He turns your place into a sugar shack."

"This could go down a little easier if you would try not to use expressions like sugar shack?" Sam took a deep drink of her wine and found it insufficient.

"One other thing. He broke off with you because he spotted his next victim. Most likely someone you introduced him to."

"You're an asshole when you want to be, but you should never have even considered retiring."

"If we are telling truths and bearing our souls, the truth is it's his loss. You are much too good for someone that is conniving. I saw you save a stranger's life today. And at no time did you fall apart." With this, Bobby stood and prepared to leave.

"Don't go. Stay the night on the sofa." It was obvious Sam had an explanation about not wanting to be alone, but it was not necessary.

Bobby lye in the night, reliving moments in his life and listening to the gentle female snoring of Sam. How could a man ever have known a sound such as this could reverse years of damage? Shake free the loneliness that had clung to his very bones. How dare I let her penetrate my shell, he thought.

Chapter 6

Scheduled on the next day were two people to be deposed. Kai Chung was scheduled for the morning, and David Donaldson was scheduled for an evening session with the judge. Bobby may have wanted to be a little more concerned that he was so rapidly becoming used to Sam as his partner, but the truth was that he had had a lot of partners, and after seeing her under pressure, he knew he could do a lot worse.

The Kai family lived in a large condo off Grand Avenue. The large stone and brick structure had been remodeled and refurbished to bring back much of olden St. Louis. A man's voice buzzed them in, and they began their ascent to the third floor.

"I hate this layout if anything goes down.

One way in. No retreat." Bobby mumbled.

"Ever the romantic partner." Sam chucked, and Bobby rethought his pessimism. When they reached the floor, a small girl of mixed Asian-American descent was peering out of a doorway at them. The little girl was gorgeous even though she looked like she may have been attacked by a jar of fresh jam. "Honey, is your mom getting ready?" Sam attempted to lean forward, and the little girl ran away. Another equally gorgeous little girl a year or so older peeped he head out of the door.

"As you most likely guessed, we don't get a lot of visitors." A tall Caucasian man appeared. He was clean-shaven and looked like he had been caught in the process of dressing for work in a major office. The little girl with the jam on her hands grabbed him by the legs and hugged fully unaware of transferring much of the jam to his pants. The man scooped the little girl up and began kissing her cheeks. "Alright, let's go get cleaned up before Mommie makes us all walk the plank." He joked with the little girl, then turned to Bobby and Sam. "You guys come in and make yourselves at home. You caught the morning rush. I'm Maxwell Kai's husband, and I take it you are her babysitters."

Maxwell was a handsome name with the ivy league look that made many women swoon. But when Kai entered the room, it was clear where the girls had inherited their good looks.

Kai Chung was electrifyingly beautiful.

She entered the room in full makeup and lit up the corners of the room where shadows would have most likely sought refuge. Upon leaving the condo, Maxwell went to kiss Kai, and she turned her head slightly so as not to smudge her makeup. A marital tell that Bobby and Sam both noticed.

"Are you married, Detective Bond?" Kai asked no sooner than the Cadillac was in motion.

Kai had insisted on sitting in the front next to Bobby, but it made little difference to Sam in that she had decided not to like this woman.

"No, I am a widower."

"Such a shame. And such a waste of such a strong strapping man." Kai commented. "But I bet you get a lot of offers. Many, I am sure, for casual encounters." Kai turned her head and let the comment sail on the wind while staring out the passenger window. Sam was unsure if Kai was just looking out the window or watching for a reflection to ascertain how her flirting with Bobby affected Sam's mood.

After lunch, where Sam said very little to Bobby, it was time to pick up David Donaldson.

Finding the North St. Louis County address was easy; that could have been an omen. Bobby and Sam walked the lane to the single-family Donaldson home, and suddenly Sam stopped and faced Bobby. She looked into his eyes to be sure she had his full attention. "Do you want the good news first or the bad news?' She asked.

"The good." Bobby relented.

"Well, that's the problem. There is no good news. Only bad and worse than bad." Sam stood facing Bobby, pretending to remove a spot from his tie.

"Spit it out, Sam."

"Well, your Asian girlfriend is back."

"I just met Kai Chung, and she is manipulative. She likes getting a rise out of people. She was getting a bigger charge out of messing with you than talking to me."

"I like hearing you say that, but I was talking about the Asian lady that was at the bank building the other day when we got this chickshit assignment."

"Oh."

"She is parked in a car off your left shoulder. Let me know when you want the really bad news."

"You must be joking. It can't get any worse than that."

"Well, boss, I can't make out the plates on her car, but they are federal tags, and she has been with us since we left the civil court building."

Bobby wiped his face as if it mattered. "Okay, I have a plan."

"Shoot."

"We catch a plane to Clearwater, rent a fishing boat, and sail out for a few months. I hear the Marlin are running this time of year."

"I don't know if I would be safe with such a big strapping man as yourself." Sam did her best to imitate Kai.

"You are jealous of her?"

"Hell yeah. She is everything I am not, and she doesn't even seem to care. She has a handsome, smart husband and a couple of the cutest kids I have ever seen. Me, I am a resting place for some guy's dick when his wife is unavailable."

Bobby grabbed Sam by the arms and shook her. "Don't you ever let me hear you talk about yourself that way?" The was a look of anger on his face. Sam was not sure how to take it. "Okay, Bobby, lighten up on the grip."

Bobby released his grip. "I am sorry. I have seen so much waste in my lifetime. Not you too. God damnit, not you too."

"Don't worry about it, Bobby. It's good to know you care. Look, we went from being enemies to being close to friends in nothing flat. Now let's go drag this sorry piece of shit in front of a judge and call it a day."

Bobby woke up the three steps to the front door and knocked. Sam went to the side of the house and investigated the house through a window. "You might have to knock a little louder." Bobby walked down the steps to see what Sam was looking at. David was seated in a chair, slumped over the table with a hole in his head. He had a large caliber pistol in one hand that rested on the table in front of him.

Sam stared at Bobby. "Clearwater, huh? That's in Florida, right?" Sam commented.

"I swear if there weren't a fed sitting fifty feet away, we would be sailing before nightfall." Sam put her arm around Bobby's shoulder. "Why don't I call the cops while you call the court clerk and tell him the game has been called on account of rain."

THE INVESTIGATING DETECTIVE was unhappy with finding a dead body, but with the house locked and no apparent break-ins and a suicide note, they were relieved there wasn't more mess. The detective tried every possible variation of the question of what he was being deposed for and why he needed to escort him. But Bobby and Sam had no answers for them.

"I am going to take you to your place so you can pack an overnight bag." Bobby whispered to Sam when the officers had released them.

"Why, what's up?"

"I have been asking around, and there may be someone who can shine a little light on this mess. The problem is I don't know him. He is the friend of a friend."

"At this pace, we had better take what we can get before we wind up dead or in jail for something we don't understand."

Sam confirmed.

"My thoughts exactly. I would go alone, but your butt is in the same wringer as mine."

"What about the next person to take to the judge's chambers?"

"We must be back in time for that; the guy we need is in Chicago. We take the train."

THE GENTLE ROCKING of the train and the dim lighting eased many of Bobby and Sam's worries. Sam seemed to dose off occasionally, but she sat next to Bobby, enjoying the ride.

"Tell me about what happened with Waylon." Waylon had been Sam's father.

"Not much to tell. The cancer started eating him up, and he said he always wore his boots like a man he was going out as a man. Blew his brains out."

Bobby could not tell if it was sadder to tell the tailor relieving to be able to release it. "And Sam, your uncle."

"Diabetes. That once big, loud barrel-chested man was little more than skin and bones in the end. Hell, I could lift him to change his adult diapers."

"I should have been there."

Bobby muttered.

"No. He did not want anyone to see him like that. He wanted to be remembered as the life of the party he always was. He loved me more than my own father." Sam seemed to be drifting back to sleep.

When Bobby and Sam reached Union Station in Chicago, a very tall woman in a Chicago police uniform stood holding a sign that read Bobby and Sam. They walked to her. "Sir and ma'am." She shook their hands. "I am Officer Cobb. I graduated at the top of my class at the academy a little over a year ago, and I have specific instructions. I am not to ask any questions or give any answers. I am to take you to your meeting and then drop you off. I am to forget I ever saw you, and if anyone ever asks me, I have no knowledge of you ever being in Chicago." She smiled, removing the stern look from her face. "God, I love this kind of shit." As Cobb led the way to the vehicle, Sam whispered to Bobby. "At least someone does."

"GOOD LUCK." COBB BID as he sped off, leaving Bobby and Sam on the sidewalk in front of the bar. The bar was closed at this hour of the morning, but a half dozen large black men were standing in front that seemed to be waiting for them.

The sign on the bar door read, "Welcome to God's Last Outpost." In small writing, it stated, "One step beyond this point, and you are on your own."

"Bobby," Sam whispered. "I don't care what happens. Don't leave me alone in here for a second."

"No worries, I won't let you out of my sight," Bobby confirmed.

"This way." Elderly black women with silver hair instructed. "Then she pointed toward the back office behind the bar."

A big man and a tough-looking black woman walked out of the office. "Show me some ID." The man commanded, staring at Bobby. Bobby pulled out his private investigator's license and handed it to the man.

"What the fuck is this. Show me your shit or take a hike." The man grunted.

"Bobby reached into his inside jacket pocket and pulled out his badge. St. Louis Metropolitan Police Detective Homicide retired.

The integrator stared at it momentarily, then showed it to the black woman with him. "Come in and have a seat. I am Detective Blake, and this charming doll is my partner Detective Carter."

"You must be his partner. You are young, but the minute you entered that door, you signed up for the big leagues." Carter's comment was as intimidating as it was meant to be to Sam, but she hoped she did not show it.

"What I am going to tell you is we have not only been ordered not to discuss, and we have been threatened with dire consequences if we reveal any of the information. Are we clear on that?" As Blake spoke, that all found seats in the small office.

"Roughly three weeks ago, we got a call in the middle of the night to go to the Congress Hotel. A four-star hotel in the convention district. When we got there, a buxom blonde girl was nude in the middle of the hotel fountain in the center of the atrium." Blake made a gesture when he started buxom, and Carter slapped his hand down.

"Who was she?" Sam asked.

"Her registration said she was Blondie Bumstead." Carter answered.

Bobby's head dropped into his hands.

"Bobby who is Blondie Bumstead?" Sam asked.

"And that is why kids don't work homicide." Carter stated in a snippy tone.

"Blondie Bumstead is Dagwoods wife. They are old-time comic strip characters." Bobby attempted to bring Sam up to speed.

"Two-night auditors heard the splash and crash. Instead of calling the police, they contacted the resident manager." Blake continued.

"What the hell is that?" Bobby asked, looking confused.

"He is a twenty-four-hour manager on duty at the big Hotel for emergencies that happen after normal business hours. And dead girls are showing up in the fountain, probably being on the shortlist." Sam added quickly, regaining her creditability with the group.

"No witnesses?" Bobby asked, seeming more exasperated.

"That, as they say, is where the plot thickens."

Carter answered. "See, the auditor thinks the girl did a naked high dive from the ninth floor. But when we arrived, the resident let everyone on the ninth floor check out and scatter to the winds."

"I certainly hope you arrested the motherfucker for obstruction of justice." Bobby ranted.

"We did, and he did a David Copperfield. Vanished into thin air all while in lock up." Carter stated.

"Thirty-one rooms," Sam stated as if it was the answer to a question someone was about to ask.

"What is she saying?" Blake asked, but Sam looked directly at him.

"There are 871 guest rooms in that Hotel. That would put about 31 on the ninth floor.

So, you get the registration for the guest on that floor." Sam stated as if it was obvious.

"All the IDs for the guest on that floor were fake." Blake stated.

Sam turned and looked at Bobby as if he was the only other person in the room. "That's impossible."

"Explain, Sam." Confidently Bobby asked.

"Because the number of people using fake IDs in hotels is directly related to the dollar value of the rooms. So, say the Hotel or motel is a cheap no-tell motel. The number is high. But with a four-star hotel, most of the rooms are booked with credit cards, and many are booked from another hotel. Still, another group is booked through rewards programs, and most of the rest are booked by companies for conventions and meetings. So that means the people entering the Hotel have already been vetted before they arrive."

"Oh shit, I think I see where you are going," Bobby stated.

"You want to let the slow learner in on it, wiz kid." Carter mocked.

"If one percent of the rooms rented were fake IDs, one percent of 871 is 8.71 rounded to nine."

"Oh shit, I missed it by getting mad about being put off the case. You are saying that there should have been no more than nine fake in rooms, not thirty-one."

Blake exclaimed.

"Not only should that, but your population of nine should have been scattered among the total population of 28 floors. There is no way those people ended up on the same floor without planning or some form of computer manipulation."

"They are one big ass group," Carter concluded. "That explains how they got out of the Hotel so fast. They knew each other well enough to assist each other depart."

Blake and Carter spent the remainder of the meeting giving their little details. The trace on the blonde had come been lost, and the toxicology report had been destroyed or misplaced. None of the alias used on that night had shown any value, but the investigation was closed an hour after Blake and Carter surrendered their case notes.

Through a system of nods and winks, Officer Cobbs's police cruiser reappeared. The large number of muscular black men that had been collected on the front of the bar turned out to be mostly off-duty cops securing the area for the meeting.

"The train station is the other way." Sam noted to Bobby as Cobb drove into a neighborhood near a school.

"Don't worry; you will make your train. You have fifteen minutes for whatever it is you are doing or not doing here." Cobb responded as she pulled the car over and assisted them from the car. Near the school was a large play area and a park.

There were many children of all ages running and jumping and having a good time. A woman in a hoodie stood by a jungle gym watching the children. It was clear to Bobby she was waiting for them.

"Let me guess; you are Ramona." Bobby guessed, offering his hand. Both Ramona and Sam looked surprised that Bobby seemed to expect her.

"Look, if this is a setup, killing me won't accomplish anything. I told you guys before that we did not see a thing. We heard the crash and saw that poor girl." Ramona's large brown eyes seemed to be tearing, remembering the scene.

"We aren't here to kill you. But any information you could help us with prove may beneficial." Sam offered a comforting tone.

"Okay, you want to know what I know here it is. Two days after the girl shows up in the fountain, I get a letter from the Hotel saying my services are no longer needed and I am not to set foot on the company property again.

In the same batch of mail is a letter congratulating me on getting a job in, of all places, Iowa. The job is with a nice hotel in an executive position. Seven-figure salary with four assistants who do the work." Ramona paused and looked around. "Now, here is the funniest part. If you gave me a map of the United States and took the names of the states off, with ten guesses, I couldn't pick out Iowa. So, there is no way in hell I applied for this job."

"A payoff," Bobby noted.

"Just as I am packing for points unknown, I get a call from a lady that says she is Hiram Wakefield's wife, and he is missing.

The last time I saw Wakefield, you cops had him in handcuffs. Now you can't find him. I don't know what kind of shit you guys have going but count me out.

I did not see anything. And even if I had, I grew up in a neighborhood where you learn the best time to keep your mouth closed. I am out of here. I am taking the job, so no one thinks I am playing Nancy Drew and misplaces my ass. The other auditor with me was Lizzy, and I can't reach her cell; it's been disconnected."

Bobby and Sam could see that Cobbs's cruiser had returned, and it was time to leave. They started walking toward the curser, and Sam stopped for a minute to wish Ramona well, but when Sam turned back around, Ramona was gone. Only the children at play remain.

"THANK YOU FOR WHAT you did in that meeting.

When the Cornel said both our skill sets would be required, I guess this is what he meant. I am only an old street cop, but you know the new." Bobby and Sam sat on the train. Sam rested herself against Bobby, not asking for permission or pretending it was an accident.

"So why a playground?" She asked.

"It was to create ambient sound and block out the use of parabolic listening devices," Bobby answered in a muttered tone that told me there was something else he wanted to say. "I was thinking that if you wanted to bail on this case, I would understand."

Sam sat up and stared directly at him. "Hold the fuck on. Bobby, if this is your way of saying you got what you need, now, it's time to wash up and go home."

"No." Bobby stopped her, grabbed her arms, remembered where he had hurt her before, and let go. "I am saying I'm starting to get scared for you."

"Say the rest of it, Bobby." She commanded, and the train clicked down the countryside.

"Now you are putting me on the spot?"

"Okay, I will make it easy for you." Sam sat back and again rested against Bobby. "If you encountered a younger version of yourself and wanted to give him advice, what would you say?'

Now it was Bobby's turn to rest back against his seat. He stared out at nothing in particular as he descended into himself. "I would say you are right ninety percent of the time and wrong ten, so stop spending ninety percent of your time worried about the ten percent.

I would tell myself to be better at taking my own advice and stop letting well-meaning but ignorant people talk me out of things I have researched." Bobby's breathing slowed for a moment. "I would tell my Michelle; I loved her every chance I got." Sam reached over and offered Bobby her hand, and he accepted it. She was not sure if he was holding Sam's hand or Michelle's, but it did not matter for the moment.

"I would tell that brass young punk to stop being such a hard ass when it comes to defining friendships and relationships."

Bobby turned and looked closely at Sam.

She knew he now saw her. "I would say someone wants to risk being your friend, take it, embrace it."

Chapter 7

L arry Walker was the next witness to be escorted to the judge's chambers, and both Sam and Bobby were eager to get through the evening. They had arrived back in St. Louis with just enough time to pick up Bobby's car and drive to the St. John home of Mr. Walker.

They were hungry, and both needed a bath, but neither complained.

Larry Walker was a tall gaunt man with long stringy hair. He looked like he was waging a war against aging and losing miserably. He was the material process manager for quality control at Sheffield Processing.

"Wait a minute, let me get my jacket." Walker reached back into the house for the jacket, and Sam heard the peeling of rubber as tires squealed. There was a black Malibu racing toward them. She noticed the driver was one of the twins. He spent the wheel of the car and removed a pistol from the passenger seat and fired. The driver then sped off. Sam jumped the railing in front of the house and ran chasing the car. It stopped and turned around and headed for her. Back in the front of the house, Bobby noticed a second car speeding toward the front of the house. A different variation of the same game, he thought. Distract and drive the person covering the client away from the target. Not this time, Bobby thought. Don't watch Sam; she will be fine, a voice screamed in his head. The second car was blue and had the same make. It raced directly toward him. Bobby pulled his gun and fired, shooting out the front tire of the car, causing it to swerve. The pop of his gun was followed by the explosion of the tire a hubcap shot off and ricocheted against a neighboring house. The driver tried to reverse, but the tail end went sideways into the muddy yard of a close home, causing the rear wheels to spin, slip, and fling mud. The driver tried to jump out of the driver's side door was jammed. The twin kicked open the passenger side of the car and exited. He looked at the angry eyes of Bobby. The twin brought his gun to bear, and Bobby shot in in the center of the forehead. Slowly Bobby walked over to the twin and kicked the gun away from his hand. Now he thought. Now it's time to check on Sam. Bobby turned around, and at her feet was a teenager that looked identical to the one at his feet down to the hole in the center of his forehead. Bobby and Sam walked toward each other. "Are you glad you didn't kick me to the curb this morning?" Sam asked.

Bobby was unable to help himself. He hugged her.

"ALRIGHT, YOU TOO, CLOWN. My boss says to give you two back your stuff and get your stinking butts out of St. John." The desk Sargent notified Sam and Bobby as they sat waiting in a holding cell. "I thought retired meant you should be somewhere playing golf."

'He promised to take me Deepsea fishing in Clearwater." Sam joked.

"Your boss wants you in his office asap, and there is some little Asian fed that said get you back on the street as so as possible. Must be nice to have pull." The sergeant bellowed.

"Pull my ass. She is using us for clay pigeons." Bobby corrected.

"Couldn't happen to a nicer pair."

"The great man awaits." Betty announced as Bobby and Sam entered the Winters and Slay office of Cornel Jack Morrison.

"He will have a coffee, black, one cream, two sugars." Sam called a secretary that was leaving the office.

"Now I know why I never got that bulldog I always wanted. The damn things never let shit go." They both found the humor in his joke at different levels.

"What have you two got so far." The authoritarian voice of Morrison corners Bobby and Sam's attention as they sit in his office facing him.

"Well, sir, that depends on whether I am talking to Cornel Jack Ironman Morrison, former seal, and the man I would trust with my life.

Or if I am talking to just another one of Winters and Slays executives." Bobby answered.

"Let's not hold back, Bobby. Not now. We might be talking to an errand boy for the feds." Sam commented. Bobby knew it was what is called in poker as an all-in shove. A bluff of epic proportions and Bobby knew the only way for it to work was to follow her lead.

"Lady, I could bounce your ass right out of here." Morrison stood and stared at Sam.

She relaxed and sat back in the chair.

"The little Asian fed that visited you the day we got this assignment and the same one we saw at the suicide." Sam continued.

Morrison sat back down for a moment. There was silence as he stared at the city skyline growing dim. When Morrison turned back around, his hand changed. He was ready to deal. "Okay, here is what I know. It's a game."

If Bobby had not seen it with his own two eyes, he never would have believed it. This mire wisp of a woman had back down former Navel Seal Commander Jack Ironman Morrison and now had him suing for peace. "What kind of game?" Bobby asked.

Morrison looked down in embarrassment. "A sex game. But I don't know how it worked or what the rules are."

"Who is Blondie Bumstead?" Sam had asked the next relevant question.

"She is or was the daughter of a US senator, and now he is on the warpath." Morrison explained.

"Why the depositions?" Sam asked.

"A sex game spanning at least two states with political pull. Not to mention Police influence."

Chapter 8

"Hey, Bobby, bring me a towel to dry off with."

Sam's apartment had a shower but no tub.

She had been soaking in bubble bath in Bobby's tub. Bobby handed her the towel from around the corner of the bathroom. He had cleaned up first on her insistence because she wanted a leisurely soak. "You can come in if you want. You have seen me naked before." Bobby chose to remain outside the bathroom and to bypass the comment.

"I got to say, Sam, I have never been prouder of a partner than when you went all in on Ironman Morrison and had him back down."

"I am just glad you understood what I was doing.

I had to do it since you two are old friends. He would have fed you information with an eye dropper and never covered what we needed."

Bobby could hear her splashing around like a little kid. "I made up the sofa for you to sleep on."

"When did we decide I was staying the night."

"I decided when you had your third or fourth glass of wine. I decide that you are not the type of person that could live with herself if she got into a car accident and someone's kid was killed, whether it was her fault or not."

"Alright, score one for you. Do you want to know what my most favorite moment was with you, Partner?" He heard her blowing bubbles as she asked.

Bobby sat on the floor with his back to the bathroom. "Tell me."

"It was when you turned around and looked at me after blasting that teenage hitman. You surveyed the area and had this look like. Yeah, that's right, me and my partner can handle some shit. Anybody else wants a piece of this."

"Is that how you saw it?"

"Bobby, your look told me you trust me as a partner.

Not as a teacher mentor or some other bull shit but someone you trust to have your back. Maybe I haven't been at this as long as you, but I know that feeling is what makes all the difference."

They were silent for a moment, not sure what to say next. Bobby hears Sam rising from the tub. "Do me a favor, Bobby. Be careful with that Asian woman."

"You are still jealous of Kai Chung?"

"Hell yeah, but I mean the other Asian woman. The fed."

"You got a bad feeling about her partner?"

Bobby inspected the slight bruises where he had grabbed her in excitement over her earlier self-deprecating statement.

"Let me answer this way. How long were you a cop?"

"Over twenty years."

"So do you think that if you were in the single largest building in St. Louis and you did not want to be seen, you could manage it?"

Sam's question rocketed home something that had been festering in the back of his mind. He had been too preoccupied with Sam being the wrong Sam and life-changing without his permission that he missed the obvious. "She is playing a game, and we are expendable."

"Maybe her target was Morrison and shaking his confidence, but either way, we can trust anything she says." Sam exited the bathroom holding the front of her towel with one hand and half an empty bottle of wine in the other. "And as for Ms. Chung, just don't stick your dick in her. She strikes me as the type that will let you then throw it in her husband's face."

In an instant after curling up on the sofa, Sam was sound asleep. Bobby waited for it. Once again, the turbulent vibration that is the inevitable result of time calmed his head, and he could relax.

Chapter 9

B obby and Sam pulled up and parked in the Webster Groves neighborhood where the home of Norman and Joan Campbell was located.

Webster Groves is another of the residential counties surrounding the city of St. Louis. Norman was the next scheduled to be deposed. No sooner than Bobby had parked the car, the Asian fed drove slowing past him and winked. It was obvious that she had followed Bobby and Sam from Bobby's house. Bobby sat for a moment, watching several small pockets of school-age kids with backpacks and books scurrying alone into their day.

"Gunfight or suicide?" Bobby asked Sam. Sam ignored the question, still watching the federal agent drive a safe distance off to watch them. "She wants to talk to you, but she doesn't want me there when she does."

"How do you know that?"

"It's a woman thing."

"Why alone?"

"Because she plans to flirt with you and make you dream of the possibly of kinky sex while she pumps you for information and fills you with misinformation."

Bobby sat back, still watching the children. He knew he did not have to tell Sam he wanted them off the streets before they walked to the house. "What did you do in the army?" Bobby asked.

"Army intel."

"That makes sense. Why even former Cornels don't shake you? That and being Sam Boone's kid."

"I am Whalen Boone's kid; remember his brother."

For the moment, Bobby wondered if he had let on the family secret slip, but Sam started talking again. "If you could tell a woman something, and you thought all women were listening, what would it be?"

Bobby thought for a moment, grateful she had created her own diversion. "First, I would say, please stop trying to make us apologize for being men. If that is what we are, that's what we are. Second, I guess I would say guys like me were programmed from early youth to be what we became. You can't go back in time and reprogram us. No latest craze or sexual revealing craze that started in the last ten years can undo and redo the programming that started twenty to thirty to forty years before that." Bobby turned to Sam and saw shock in her face at his candor. "I guess you have been thinking about this for a little while."

"It's an old guy thing. Now the street is clear enough, let's keep our fingers crossed that this is a dull, boring pickup."

The home of Norman and Joan Campbell is immaculate in an almost scary way. There were large purple flowers, and pastel colors worked into patterns on much of the décor. The type of thing most men would have fought to their death to prevent. Joan was a skinny unattractive woman who smoked non-filtered cigarettes, clutching them in her thin, talon-like, yellowing fingers.

She walked directly up to Sam and released a blast of secondhand smoke. "You taking this one to testify too. Marshal?"

"No, she is my partner. And since I saw her kill a guy less than twenty-four hours ago who was nicer to her than you. You might want to watch where you are blowing that smoke. Where did you get those anyway, a gun store? I thought those were outlawed."

"Come on, Romeo?" Sam stated to Norman as he entered the room. She hooked her arm under Normans and made a point of bumping Joan with her shoulder as she escorted the pail-thin Norman from the house.

"Bobby, do you mind if Norman and I ride together in the back? I think we need some quality time together." Sam stated, pushing Norman into the back seat, and then sliding next to him. Sam then waved at Joan. As they drove off, you could hear Joan scream. "Don't forget where you got the loan bitch."

As Bobby slowed down to dive past the Asian fed, Sam gave an overly aggressive wave from the back seat.

"You are an even bigger sit starter than your uncle." Sam mumbled.

"I love you too, Bobby but Norman and I need some special time together."

Norman began to sweat. And not a mild sweat. It was raining sweat. "Tell me about the game, Norman."

"We aren't supposed to talk about it. It's one of the rules." Norman's voice shook.

"Norman baby people are dying. I don't want to see you become one of them. Let's say we talk and then pretend we never did." Sam leaned forward to address Bobby. "That all right, you, Bobby?"

"Sure, sounds like the best for all involved. If we can save this guy's ass, we do."

Sam leaned closer. "Must be your cologne that is attracting Asian bitches, but that fed is following, and this time, I don't think she cares that we know she is there."

"Great."

As Bobby Cadillac entered Highway 64/40 with the fed closely following, Sam sat back in the seat. "Now, Norman, explain a little about how it works. The sex games."

"Well, let's say you are a pretty normal person. You got married at an early age. Most of your life has been spent working and planning your family. You missed out on the fun a lot of people had on a regular basis."

"So, what is the club about?"

"Let's say you want to experiment a little. You know, have sex with a woman other than that shrew that is draining the life out of you. So, you think wife swapping, but no one on this or any other planet would want that nasty tobacco bug in exchange for a normal woman."

The loss for word was clear on Sam's face. She allowed Norman to continue. "The game master sets you up with a partner. A woman that is like a surrogate wife for wife-swapping purposes, and the two of you attend functions and affairs."

"Norman, you make this sound so civilized." Those where the first words Sam could come up with.

"It has been. Everyone is vetted. That means regular health checks and the Game Master tells you when and where to go to get a checkup. Anyone can say no to anything. Guys are matched to a girl, and they watch out for each other. If a guy gets out of hand, all the guys must act.

"Wrap it up. We are running out of time." Bobby singled from the front seat, letting Sam know the interrogation had to end soon they were reaching their destination.

"Who is the Game Master?" Sam asked.

"I don't know, and no one I ever talked to says they know."

"How did this start?"

"Well, about three years ago, there was a big convention in New York. A bunch of people from various parts of the industry got together. Some people who had been only talking together via the phone and email met for the first time. The story goes that after the party a sort of orgy broke out, and someone had the idea to systemize the process and have a sex club."

"Hold on." Bobby sounded from the front seat. "Three years ago. You are saying this sex club had been underground for three years."

"Hold on, Bobby; I got a better question. Were you in Chicago when Blondie Bumstead died?"

Norman looked down as if the answer was there.

"Yes, but sorry to say I was wedged in between two two-hundred-pound Iowa farm girls turned machine operator. All I can remember is someone telling me we all had to get our shit and split."

After dropping off Norman with two Deputies to take him into the judge's chambers, Bobby and Sam ran into the Asian Fed that had been following them. She was barely five feet tall but filled the space blocking their path with a large coat of tuberous.

"Samantha, do you mind if I speak privately with your partner?" Jay J. Kahn flashed her FBI badge.

"Well, yes, I mind, but it's up to him."

"Aren't we civil all of a sudden."

"I want her to stay; see, basically, I am just another knuckle-dragging caveman, and she is my only link to this century."

"So, what have you learned so far?" Kahn led.

"We learned that we are simple escorts." Sam said in a mocking voice.

Kahn gave Sam a quick angry glance. "Look, I helped expedite your release; the least you could do is do some professional courtesy."

"Okay, you want professional courtesy. Let's play; you show me yours; I show you mine." Bobby offered.

"That's more like what I had in mind until you insist the kid stay close by." Khan said in a sultry voice.

"Told you she would play the tramp card the first chance she got."

"Watch your mouth, Samantha." Khan closed the distance between the two women in the busy court building hallway.

"Or what, Jay? Are you going to make me disappear like poor Hiram Wakefield? And for the record, that one is a freebie." Sam stood her ground.

"Damn, you guys are coming up fast." Kahn comment. "Alright, here is one for the two of you. The dispositions are to determine corporate liability for the death of the Senator's daughter."

"Now, that is a new one on me." Sam stared at Bobby because of his comment. Sam put her hand on his arm. "What am I missing."

"Don't you see it? In this country, there are basically two different court systems, civil and criminal. Usually, people go to the civil when they feel total justice has not been served in criminal court. Here it's the other way around. Someone is squeezing those companies through civil litigation to force them to come up with the killer."

"If there is even a killer. Do you know what a steeple chase is?" Kahan asked.

"Yeah, a race with a bunch of deliberate obstacles."

"Welcome to the steeplechase." Kahn said as she handed Bobby her card and walked away.

Sam stood with her back to Bobby as Agent Kahn sashayed away. "Bobby, if I turn around and you are watching that tight little butt of her, I am going to be so upset."

"Sam."

"Yes."

"Let's go find lunch before we have to drive Norman home."

BOBBY AND SAM WENT out to dinner and had a long talk. They talked not only about the case but about how times have changed. Bobby found Sam's laugh exhilarating. She was different. She was life itself. At Bobby's house, she sat on the sofa in a half-light room, drinking a small glass of whiskey. Sam walked into the room wearing one of his old police department tee shirts. She straddled his legs and sat on him with her arms around his neck. Sam leaned forward, allowing her hair to fall forward. She kissed Bobby slightly. Bobby held him back to make eye contact.

"No, Sam. I don't think so."

"You are telling me my uncle never gave you a lap dance." She giggled.

"No one had that much lap."

"Then tell me I am wrong that you don't feel for me like I feel for you."

There was a gentle pleading to Sam's tone now. She just wanted the answer. She needed it.

"Yes. Samantha, I feel what you feel, but it's bad business for partners to get involved."

Sam began rocking her hips. "You are involved."

"Good to know everything is still working the way it should."

"Oh shit. I'm sorry. God, I can be such a dumb ass at times." Sam hugged Bobby. "I should have taken the clue from when we were coming back on the train."

Bobby looked at her knowing she was about to expose his heart.

"You are still in love with your late wife.

It hurt you to say her name to me the other day. It was like saying her name to another woman was a form of cheating." Sam knew by the look on his face she had found the reason he struggled with being so close to her. "Look, Bobby, I've never been on this side of the equation. Telling someone I love you, just trust me."

"God, what makes us what we become." Bobby uttered as she rose from his lap.

"Don't worry, Bobby, we got time."

There was a knock on the door. "You are expecting anyone?" Sam asked.

"You mean like late-night Jehovah's Witnesses."

Sam retrieved her gun and followed Bobby to the door.

Bobby opens the door slowly with his gun hidden behind his back. A tall thin, gaunt man in an extremely expensive suit stood there. There was also a man that looked like a bodybuilder in an equally impressive suit on his left and a female bodybuilder in a suit on his right. Bobby looked out the door and noticed the stretch limo poorly parked in front of his house.

"My name is Astrachan. These are my associates, Mr. Seven and Ms. Eight. May we come in? There are a couple of matters we would like to discuss that I am sure you will find lucrative." Astrachan spoke in a slow southern accent. Not the uneducated Southern draw often made fun of by comics but a refined Southern accent that sounds like it had been passed from generation to generation. "I assure you if you feel comfortable with your firearms at the ready, you make keep them so." The man calling himself Astrachan smiled a smile that radiated confidence and foretold of advance planning.

"Sure, but this is a residential neighborhood with limited parking space. Would you mind asking your driver to pull up to the cul-de-sac and wait? I would want one of the kids just learning to drive to tag your rear bumper."

"You are Robert Bond, former Homicide Detective working as a private investigator for the Winters and Slay Law firm." He then turned to Sam. "And this lovely young lady must be Samantha Boone, formally of Kansas City police and Army Military Intelligence."

Astrachan made his announcements as if making a boardroom presentation. He made no mention of Mr. Seven or Ms. Eight.

"It's getting late. How can we help you?" Bobby tried to filter some of the annoyance out of his voice.

"It has come to my attention that you are searching along a path that may be beneficial to my employer." A moment of silence passed then Sam spoke. "He is waiting for us to mention the game."

"Beauty and brains, I bet many have made the mistake of underestimating you. I will try not to follow in their footsteps." He paused for effect. "Yes, the game. We were thinking that should we pool our resources; it may be a quicker means to an end."

"That might work if our goals were the same and we could all live with the outcome, but I don't think our goals are the same."

Bobby assessed.

"Perhaps not, but you may find the answer we are searching for before us, and if you turn that information over to the feds, it will not serve us well."

"It's been a long day, and this shitty case that was supposed to be a drop in the bucket is getting shittier by the moment, so just so I am clear, was that a threat." Bobby eyed the bodyguards.

"Threats are a waste of time at an inappropriate time.

It is an offer. One million dollars if you can get us what we need. That is one million dollars any way you want it on the record or in a trash bag dropped on your doorstep."

"We need some time to think about it. We had been discussing some Marlin fishing off the coast of Clearwater." Sam injected.

Astrachan reached into his inside pocket and removed a picture. "This is a picture of Tracy Atwater before her demise."

Both Bobby and Sam stepped forward to view the picture. No one seemed to care that Sam was dressed only in a men's tee shirt and panties. Or that Bobby and Sam were still holding handguns. The picture was a young, fresh-faced Tracy in a cap and gown.

"I was almost expecting a photoshopped picture of her in a girl scout uniform holding a box of those really hard cookies they sell." Sam commented, and Astrachan clearly allowed the dig to pass.

"Maybe everyone can get what they want in this." Astrachan remarked.

Bobby watched Astrachan leave as mysteriously as he appeared. When he turned around, Sam was dressing. "Where are you going."

"Home. I don't live here, and you have some thinking to do."

"And if I ask you to stay. If I beg you to stay."

"On the sofa or in your bed? Maybe I am not as good with rejection crap as I thought."

"Sam, you were right. I still get visits from the ghost of my wife. And I can't apologize for that. And a big part of me is reminded that you are somewhere at the beginning of something; I am somewhere near the end of it."

"So, I guess the question is, do you think I am worth pushing a few old rules aside? I am falling in love with you, Bobby, and I don't think there is room in your bed for me and your wife, let alone some antiquated rulebook. I didn't know her, but I don't think she would deny you a chance to live."

Sam's answer can be in the form of a kiss that had been suspended in a romantic haze and wanting to be shared. The kiss led them to the bedroom, where not only did their bodies intertwine, but so did care, concern, and love.

Sam popped up in bed in the middle of the night.

Bobby waken to see what had shocked her awake.

"What time is it?" Sam asked.

Bobby looked at the clock. "It's 2:15, and we have two pickups in the morning and new players. We need our rest.

"No, Bobby, it's not. I must have been blocked sexually, and you freed the block."

"Just doing my job, ma'am, but what are we talking about?" Sleepily Bobby asked.

"I have an idea about another part of the steeplechase. Remember I said that there is no way randomly 31 rooms on the same floor could be booked by anonymous people."

Bobby moved to a seated position. "Right, something about the law of random chance."

"Well, my dear blockbuster." She kissed his shoulder before continuing. "When you see the time on the clock, it says 2:15 because that is how you perceive time.

Really there is a long never-ending decimal attached to that time. Everything behind the decimal point is called the Matias."

"So."

"So, when we were talking about booking rooms, we were assuming a group of 31 couples booking on their home computers. That would have connected to the resignation computer, and their rooms would have been assigned all over the Hotel."

"But they were not. And now you know why."

"Because they were booked at the same time from one computer. One with the ability to calculate even faster and beyond the reservation's computer."

"I must be getting smarter after having sex with you, but I think I see your point. The Game Master booked the rooms using the manufacturing process computers from one of the companies involved."

"Well, if that is the case, here is the rub. Tonight, our mystery guest said something about everyone getting what they want. The civil court wants to know if the companies were liable for that girl's death.

He wants the Game Master's ass. I only wish we knew more about Astrachan."

"We will when I told him to move the limo to the cal de sac. Well, that is where Mrs. Reed lives. She is our neighborhood watch person. She writes down the number of cars she doesn't recognize parking on the block and gives it to me. By midday, we will know more about Astrachan than his grandmother.

Now go back to sleep, and please stop dreaming in numbers."

Chapter 10

The next person to pick up was Shannon Clarke.

She was an athletically built black woman with natural hair. She had an engaging smile highlighted by equally engaging large eyes. Bobby walked around the Clarke apartment, waiting for Shannon to get prepared, eyeing the many athletic event photos of her and the man he assumed to be her husband. The man was a strong black man in various athletic uniforms. There were trophies and plaques on his achievements.

"You might recognize my husband, Ronell. He played pro for a while." Shannon appeared behind Bobby, standing dangerously close. "He had a knee injury. He can do everything normal just fine, but for the pro level, that's another thing."

"What do you do for Sheffield, if I might ask."

Sam asked, hoping Shannon would remember she, too, was in the room.

"Mostly computer stuff. I help the big guys seem smarter than they really are." She bragged, then turned back to Bobby. "My husband should still be playing, but he is afraid of the drugs to keep the pain down.

He a sissy in that respect."

Both Sam and Bobby noticed that marital put-downs seemed to be prevalent in this group, but they said nothing. "You are a big strong guy. I bet there is nothing wrong with your knees. And you are even better looking than Kai said."

"What else did Kia say?" Bobby asked.

"That you let her ride up front."

Bobby and Sam sat on a bench outside the judge's chamber, waiting to take Shannon back home, and Sam asked. "Bobby, I know I don't own you after a single night of passion, but would you mind if the next time that bitch touches or rubs up against you, I punch her in the face."

"Not really a good idea. She slipped me an email address."

"I know I saw her give you something. I was wondering if you planned to tell me." Sam looked at Bobby, more vulnerable than he had ever seen her. Even the emotional crash she seemed to be on when he met her in the elevator after being dumped did not compare.

"I know a kid I used to work with on the job who does cyber-crime. I want him to take a look and see what he can find out."

"Good, then. I will hold off slugging her for the time being."

The evening pick-up was a guy named Floyd Golden.

Floyd was a wiry guy with no discernable muscular frame. He worked the Raw Material Flow, and that was the most usable information Bobby and Sam were able to collect. It was not that Floyd was quiet. Quite the contrary, he talked constantly. He talked about sports. Baseball, basketball, football, and hockey statics were committed to Floyd's memory.

When he hand seem to have brought you up to date on the pro team, he began reciting the college stats and knew all the names of the past college players on any team, past, present, or future.

Bobby and Sam had to stop by her apartment and pick up more things so she could continue to stay at Bobby's house. By the time Bobby and Sam made it to Bobby's house, the sun and gone down, and they were both showing signs of wear. When they got out his Bobby's Cadillac, a man stepped out of a parked car and started walking toward them. Simultaneously Bobby and Sam went for their guns. "Don't shoot." The voice was barely recognizable. It was Detective Blake. He stood for a moment, waiting with his hand out to his side, waiting for them to recognize him.

"I hope the two of you are hunger." Blake announced.

"I am starving." Sam called back.

"Get in your car and follow me. Dinner and a show have been arranged."

Bobby and Sam followed Blakes's rental car to a motel in East St. Louis. East St. Louis is a small city on the Illinois side of the Mississippi River. It was clear that Blake had already paid for a room.

Blake walked to a dark corner of the rundown motel and stood in front of one of the doors.

"No offense, Detective Blake, if your partner Carter is in there, and this is a foursome, I don't want to play." Sam stated, totally unsure why they were there. Slowly Blake opened the door, and there was Detective Carter standing in front of her, seated on the bed, a man and woman.

"Well, Samantha, how do you feel about a six-way?" Blake asked.

"Bobby and Sam, I want you to meet Hiram Wakefield and his concubine Lizzy." Carter announced. "Now get in here and close the door. The barbecue is getting cold."

Hiram sat timidly, shaking on the bed with Lizzy's arm around him.

"Oh, let me take a guess based on countless years of police work." Bobby asked, and Carter and Sam started preparing the barbeque buffet. "You guys arrested him for obstruction and gave him his one phone call. This yoyo does not call his wife he calls Lizzy his mistress. She bails his ass out. Then the same paperwork fairies that misplaced Tracey's toxicology report lost his release form. It was assumed he was bailed out by his wife, but when the wife is questioned, she has no blooming idea where he is."

"Meanwhile, he is shacked up in Lizzy's basement where they have been playing hid the salami while I have had every cop in Chicago looking for them on their own time." Blake updated.

Sam looked for a moment like she had been gut punch listening to the tale. "Hey, if you had a pair of testicles, you would know if you disappeared the hour after some whore takes a nine-story skydive without a word, you would set off all kinds of alarms." Sam smacked Hiram in the back of the head with her open palm.

"Stop her. She is evil, and he has great testicles."

Lizzy cried out.

Everyone looked at Sam for a moment. "Don't you all get it? He isn't a victim. He is the inside man. Even if you could tick the computer with a greater computer into booking the rooms with fake IDs on the same floor, The is always the human factor." She walked close to Hiram. "Three years, so how long ago did you spot the game? And instead of telling your bosses something was up, you ask to be a part of the debauchery."

"It wasn't debaucheries. Do you realize before this, there want a single incident? No one caught as much as a cold from anyone." Hiram confessed.

"Gee Bobby, I don't know, but if your partner gets any meaner, we are going to have to make a Chi-Town Detective out of her."

Carter said, and Blake and Bobby found themselves laughing.

"What do you two plan to do with Romeo and Juliet?"

Carter asked, taking a break from per barbeque chicken.

"I thought they were yours." Bobby stated.

"We are still in the room." Lizzy squeaked.

"I say we give them to Astrachan as a down payment. While he and his untouchables are fileting them, it will buy us time to close out this mess." Sam suggested.

"Isn't Astrachan the name of that gangster lawyer go-between who solves shit for the politicians?" Blake asked.

"One and the same is our newest best bud."

Sam stated, scarfing down a salad.

"Are you people even human?" Hiram asked.

"Look who's talking. Okay, I say we stash them at Sam's place, and I have a few buddies that can babysit. That means, for the time being, you move in with me." Bobby stated to Sam.

"Good, they can't show up in Chicago just yet. That would cause a mess." Blake agreed.

Carter leaned over to Sam and whispered. "Stop pretending to be so surprised. We both know you have already started bridging that age gap in a big way."

Sam tried to hide her blushing. Being a vegetarian, she laid claim to the large fresh salad and a large portion of the potato salad.

"Who was Tracy's partner?" Bobby asked the couple huddled on the bed. "Look, we know the two of you joined in the action whenever possible. Judging from Tracy's description, there is no way you missed out on that ride. Unless my partner is right, and you just don't have any testicles."

Carter began chuckling while Sam sat and vicariously enjoyed the chicken that Bobby was devouring during his questioning.

"He called himself Thor. But he didn't have much hammer, if you get my drift." Lizzy stated, then looked apologetically at Hiram. "Not like you, baby." Again, she paused. "I never saw him light up, but he stank of cigarette smoke to beat the band."

"Where is the Game Master?" Sam asked.

"I have no idea; I have never been near either company personally." Hiram answered.

"That's why I wasn't asking you." Sam snapped, and the other investigators looked at her, this time more willing to allow her latitude. She had proven her interrogation method varied from theirs. "Lizzy, you said you are a night auditor. So, all the books, in accounting terms, would have been closed. But to check out thirty-one rooms, you had to manually make an adjustment. That adjustment told you the bank that was responsible for the final payment. Even if they paid in advance." Sam looked at Bobby, who was clearly following her and keeping up. "Just in case something is stolen or broken in the room. We also know the room had to be booked in a single transaction to make the reservation think it was one booking, fake reservation, not thirty-one."

"The address for the bank was One Metropolitan Square." Lizzy answered as if the answer had been pulled out of her.

"We now know the Game Master is in St. Louis.

The Iowa company used a bank in New York as their primary bank. Bobby and I went over the prospectus for both companies' days ago. That explains why Astrachan, and his band of merry men are in town. They know all roads lead to St. Louis. But who or what leads them here?"

"Or at least the next bump on the steeplechase." Bobby remarked.

"I take it back. She is too smart for a Chi-Town Dick. She would make the rest of us look bad." Carter stated starting to clean up the indoor picnic.

Chapter 11

The following day was Saturday, and no one was to be escorted. Bobby knew he had slept a little late, enjoying the slight sound of a gentle Missouri rain falling outside. The light that bounces into the room, filtered by his drapes, sets a restful ambiance. And Sam was sleeping nude with her arm across him like she was trying to keep him from pulling away. Bobby could feel a vibration. Or maybe he was imagining it. It was the beating of her heart. He knew he was in love. Different than the love he shared with his wife. But somehow, this love seemed to give him back some of what had been slowly taken by the Spector of aging. He swam in her youth and saw no need to apologize to anyone. Especially himself.

The rain continued, and Sam and Bobby found it good. There was no need to make up an excuse to stay around the house on a day off.

Bobby displayed his cooking skills, and Sam plied him with knowledge of better eating habits. Somewhere near, midday, a knock came at the door. When Sam opened the front door, the muscle-bound woman that had accompanied Astrachan a couple of nights before stood holding an umbrella over shorter women with oversized eyeglasses. The woman looked shaky, like she had been crying for days and had run out of tears.

"This is Josie. Mr. Astrachan wants her to speak to you to help you decide which side of thing you are on." The female bodybuilder had just the voice you would have expected, much heavier than most women but not manly. "We will return in a half hour for her." The bodyguard left Josie shivering and looking pathetic in general. Sam rushed to Josie with a bath towel and began helping her dry off.

"I know it's early, but do you happen to have a little something to drink around here?" Josie asked.

Bobby put a little Canadian whiskey in a glass and handed it to Josie, leading her to be seated. Josie drank the whiskey in a gulp and held the glass out to be refilled.

"Who are you, Josie, and what part do you play in this mess?" Sam began.

"Well, I guess you could say I am David Donaldson, another wife. Though totally unofficial."

"You were his date for the couple swapping games."

Bobby sought to define while using a term palatable to the small group.

"You seem like nice people, so I will do my best to explain what I can but keep in mind I loved David with all my heart, and now he is dead, and I want people to pay the piper."

Bobby and Sam looked at each other, not clear whose turn it was to lead the questions. "You have a husband, is that correct? I mean one other than David."

Josie smiled a little for the first time since entering the home. She drank a little more, then sat back. "My husband is Chester. And he isn't a bad guy. He is good in many ways. We were so much alike when we met that dating and marriage seemed destiny."

"What changed?" Sam asked, seating herself on the sofa next to Bobby.

"You have a nice home, Sir." Josie looked at Bobby. "You have been married before."

"Yes. I am widowed." Bobby wanted to head off any questions that might be inappropriate.

"When people get married, they change. Hopefully, they change and grow together for the best. I went to night school while working day in that hot ass plant. I bettered myself, and I was granted a much better job with better pay. No one gave me shit. There were times when we only had one vehicle, and Chester needed it, so I walked to work or caught public transportation while so pregnant that my feet were swollen, and every step caused me to scream out in pain," She drank more brew. "Chester changed too. He gained at least 100 pounds of loose fat every year for each year we have been married. He grew a raggedy-ass beard. And please explain one thing to me, Sir. But I guess I can understand that a man can grow a mustache that blends into his beard, but how the hell do you get your eyebrows to join in on the fun? When I look around this house, I see traces of a woman other than the one seated next to you. That means you showed your wife respect and mourned her a bit. Maybe in some ways, you still do. How can anything I did show any greater disrespect for another human than transforming into whatever Chester is becoming."

"Forgive me for asking, but what about divorce?"

Sam asked, cuffing her arm under Bobby for support.

"Not really an option nowadays. I am more like a mother to him than a wife. I don't think he could survive a week without help. But I tell you what. This man here is a mighty good-looking man; why don't we say trade? You take Chester the bear, and I get good-looking here. Not a fair trade. I understand, but I am willing to throw in four of the laziest, fattest, and dumbest kids Iowa has to offer as a bonus."

"Josie, why are you here?" Bobby asked.

"Because those gangsters want to deliver the heads of the bastards that are responsible for David's death to their boss, and they seem to feel you are going to stop them by beating them to the answer to this little puzzle. I am here to beg you to let them kill the bastards. That whore Tracy was loaded doing a strip tease, and her fat ass lost he balance in her grand finale. It was unfortunate, but it was an accident." Josie burst into inconsolable tears.

"And you still want blood." Sam asked.

"I want David back, but since I can't have that, I will take a pound of whoever's flesh I can. And your time is up." Josie finished the whiskey and walked to the door to be retrieved by Astrachan's group.

"LOOK, KAI, I WILL BE the first to say I had a bunch of fun, but we need to find a way to pull the plug on the thing. Who knew it would grow so fast or last so long." Shannon Clarke sat in the back of the dimly light bar with Kia Chung, trying to plan their best move.

"If those want to be baby gangsters have done their job." Kia started, and Shannon interrupted. "Look, sugar tits, not all black people are from rat-invested ghettos. I come from a middle-class neighborhood, the same as you. They were the best I could do."

"You never seem to have any problem finding drugs."

"Sports contacts is like having a built-in pipeline."

"So, you are more like a lion in the zoo than one in the wild."

"Kia, I love fucking you, but you got some screwed-up ideas about people at times." Shannon had been offended.

"I like doing you too, baby, but it is a shame we could not have added your husband to the list of players. I get chill thinking about your man."

"Buy a sweater. He uses so many over-the-counter muscle relaxers that he is about to relax right out of a marriage. He relaxed a big part. And I do mean a big part in every aspect of why we got married."

Kai sipped her drink.

"The judges are going to rule at any moment.

When they rule, there will be a massive audit by an outside firm. We have no choice but to dump as many files as possible." Kai recommended. "That fucking Japanese FBI agent has an idea what she is looking for. God, I hate the Japanese."

Shannon looked at Kai, a little confused.

"It's a history thing."

"I FEEL LIKE WE ARE being called to the principal's office," Sam stated as she and Bobby rode the elevator in One Metropolitan Plaza. Betty called them and told them to come to Morrison's office as soon as possible.

"The only thing I can think about is how annoying you were the first time I met you in this elevator," Bobby confessed.

"Somehow, I feel like I made a lifetime's worth of choices in less than a week." She smiled. "And choosing to be with you is the best of the best."

The shock came when Bobby and Sam entered Morrisons' office. There in a chair was Agent Jay Kahn. She sat comfortably, wearing a short skirt that revealed her legs. "Now we are all one big happy family."

Morrison looked even more strained than in his last meeting with Sam. "It's over.

The escort service has been successfully completed."

"What's that mean?" Sam asked.

"Well, dear, it means the judges in Missouri and Iowa courts have heard everything they need to make a ruling. No more depositions are required." Kahn answered.

"It must also mean that they agree with the findings. So, you want to tell us what they are? Do we wait for Monday?" Bobby asked.

"Well, Bobby, since you ask so nicely, I will let you peep up my skirt. Missouri and Iowa have found that sufficient evidence has been proven to warrant a trial. Sheffield Processing and Richmond Materials Processing are being named as defendants in the wrongful death suit brought forth by the family of Tracy Atwater. The suit is set at 280 million dollars."

"Wow, that's a lot for a dead whore." Sam commented.

Morrison shot her an angry look.

"I agree, but here is the icing. Criminal charges are pursued even as we speak. On Monday, a team of FBI agents will pull all paperwork from two Chicago police departments. The hotel is being looked at for its participation. And possible murder charges for the death of Hiram Wakefield may be filed."

"Don't," Sam said.

"Don't what?" Kahn asked.

"Don't do any of it unless you want the FBI to look stupid. But especially don't file charges of murder against the Chicago Police for Hiram." Bobby stated.

"Because we had dinner with him last night," Sam added.

Morrison sat in his chair and put his head in his hands.

"You knew he was presumed dead, and you hid him. If he isn't dead, he is a murder suspect."

"No murder, at least not at the hotel," Sam said.

"The girl in the fountain."

"She did a strip that involved her dancing on the hotel railing and losing her balance. She was loaded with booze and drugs. I know her father, the senator from a conservative state, doesn't what you to pull the lid off of that." Sam stated.

"It's more than that, Sam. Remember, this is a steeplechase, and everyone wants what they want.

The beautiful agent Kahn wants a way to audit the Chicago Police. The senator wants the person or persons that set up the sex parties and drugs for his little girl. And the Cornel wants Winters and Slay happy." Bobby outlined.

"What about the hotel?" Kai asked whether you think they should get off scot-free.

"Another computer violated their computer.

Correct me if I am wrong, but shouldn't the FBI be interested in people who can invade US computer systems for fun and profit rather than opening the door for frivolous lawsuits?" Sam asked.

"What does it all matter anyway? The assignment is over, and you have no idea who the Game Master is anyway."

Bobby and Sam left the office, trying not to smile too much at Morrisons' last statement.

"OH, GIRL, NO MATTER how often you do that, you make my eyes whirl." Kai confessed to Shannon as the two women lay naked on the bed, coming up for air during an intense love-making session. They had checked into a local motel and were enjoying each other. A knock came at the door of the motel.

"Who is it," Shannon called out.

"Room service." A woman's voice called back.

"We didn't order anything," Shannon explained.

"Yeah, I know it's a complimentary bottle of wine for some store opening in the neighborhood. You must pick red or white."

"Can you just leave one at the door?" Shannon asked.

"Not with State liquor laws being what they are. A kid gets this, and it's my ass. Look, forget it. I got a lot more doors to knock on." The woman's voice sounded like she was already walking away.

"No, wait," Kai called out and raced to the door covering only her breast with a towel she had grabbed from the floor. When she opened the door, there stood Bobby and Sam.

"Damn." Greedy bitch you should have let her walk away. Shannon insulted.

Bobby and Sam sauntered into the room and closed the door behind them.

"You owe me five bucks," Sam said to Bobby, then looked at Shannon, trying to cover her naked body. "See, I bet him that neither of you whores spoke to me enough for me to need to disguise my voice."

"I'm good for the five. I plan to come into quite a bit of money real soon."

"Look, it's not what it looks like," Kai stated, searching the unmade bed for her panties.

Sam spotted them on the floor, picked them up, and handed them to her. "Sure, it is you trifling sluts, but we are not here to pass judgment."

"This caused Bobby to chuckle."

"Look, you want in. Unlimited sex in the finest hotel. Free booze and dope." Shannon made a last-ditch sales pitch.

"The thought of either of you witches touching Bobby makes me want to burn every last hair off your bodies with a blow torch." Sam stared at them.

"You see, the way it worked is the other night, Sam and I had a little disagreement. She seemed to think you were the Game Master."

Bobby pointed at Shannon. "I said no, it has to be Kai because the money for the room had to be balanced so the company never got wiser."

"That's when we realized the Game Master isn't one person. It's the both of you."

"What are our options? Is it cash you want? I mean, we must purge the books. We could divert some cash your way." Kai asked, and Shannon looked in total agreement.

"No, we were fired today, and we are a little upset about that. I mean, no one should be fired for doing their job and being shot at when the people that committed the crimes go free." Sam said in a cold tone.

"What is the bottom line?" Shannon asked in a somber tone.

"Glad you asked?" Bobby took Agent Kahn's card from his pocket and laid it on the nightstand. "Monday morning, you will go to this agent and confess all your crimes."

"That gives you tomorrow Sunday to prepare your actual spouses for the shit storm coming down the pike. And since God loves Sunday, I suggest you don't waste it." Sam stated over the sound of Kai muttering, "Evil bitch."

"That I am. But here is the kicker, as they say. We are on our way to turn your names over to the gangsters that represent the deceased girl's father, and if the FBI isn't convinced to tuck you two away, some were safe and sound; your asses, as they say, are grass."

When Sam and Bobby were driving away on the street, Sam turned to Bobby and asked. "Do you think they will do the smart thing and turn themselves in?"

"No. They will make a run for it. But that's not our problem, is it?"

Chapter 12

"Sam drug a duffel bag up the gangplank of the rental Boat in Clearwater, Florida. Bobby had been busy laying in provisions for their journey. The weather never seemed clearer and more cooperative than it did this morning. Sam picked up a brochure that had a picture of Boats, and there was marked with a sticky note that had a phone number written on it. "So, is this the one?" Sam asked her as soon as they set sail. "Yep, that's our new boat. We just have to name her." Bobby sat next to Sam. Sam had taken the cast-off time to slip into a string bikini. She handed Bobby a bottle of suntan lotion. "Bobby, I really like the way you say we in a sentence." She smiled and kissed him lightly. He turned her so he could begin applying the lotion to the back. "How did you know I wouldn't just keep going when I went to pick up the money?" Sam asked, looking slightly over her shoulder. Sam lie down on a towel on the deck, and Bobby quickly relieved her of the top of the bikini.

"You miss the point. I had a dream the other night.

I was walking along a beach with Michelle beside me, holding hands. You were seated on the porch in front of us. Michelle smiled and nodded for me to take the rest of the journey with you.

When I reached the porch, I turned around just in time to see Michelle disappear. I don't care if I have a million dollars if I don't have you too."

He touched the marks on her area where he had bruised her. "The bruise is almost gone."

"What if I want to keep them?"

"Why?"

"As a constant reminder that no matter how self-pitting I might get, someone loves me more than I love myself." Sam sat enjoying the massage portion of the lotion application for a while before speaking.

"Bobby, can I ask you a favor?"

"Anything."

"When we get our boat, can we name her Michelle?"

"Why you never knew her."

"I know, but I am grateful to her. That which makes us what we are is based on who we allow into our lives. Everything you are. Everything programmed into you is there because of the love the two of you shared."

Just as it has been the duty of lighthouses for hundreds of years to guide ships safely into harbors. Thank you for allowing us at the Looking Glass Lighthouse to steer your thoughts dreams and imagination safely to a port of enjoyment.

We are pleased that you have chosen to join us on this journey.

Please feel free to send feedback, questions, and comments to Lookingglasslighthouse@gmail.com and be sure to make your preferred literature vendor aware of your experience.

As a special thank you for allowing us to entertain you we would like to give you a special sneak peek into a due to be released soon work by Alex Mitchell. Man Among the Missing

Chapter One

Mosses rushed into the Eastern Star Cleaners.

Marta was business waiting on an elderly lady that seemed confused about her change.

"Yes, ma'am, this is the correct amount."

"I guess I must have thought it cost less. Did you raise your prices?" The old woman asked in an accusatory tone.

Mosses looked shaken, and it was clear to Marta that he wanted to talk to her. Jacob, the other person that worked with them at the cleaners, noticed the agitation in Mosses and grew nervous. Mosses did much of the pressing in the shop and seemed never to look up from his work in customers were in the store.

"No, ma'am, we have not raised any prices in over two years.

All our customers would go to the larger cleaner if we did."

The old woman gathered her goods and gave a slight smile as if that was the answer she wanted to hear.

"You have got to contact the handler and pull the plug on this operation." Mosses pleaded as the three gathered in the small office in the rear of the cleaners.

"Has our cover been blown? What did you learn at the mosque today?" Jacob asked, dropping the fake middle eastern accent he used for his cover.

"No, my cover was not blown. In fact, I now know where the bank we are looking for is located.

The man I have been shadowing was there today, and I have his trust." Mosses swallowed and gasped like he was having trouble breathing. There was clearly more to be said, but the rush of information was overwhelming.

"Then this is good news." Marta defined.

"Not at all. The reason he trusts me is that they have been following us, and they believe we are genuine terrorists because the is a federal team watching us too.

"Protection?" Marta hypothesized.

"He says they look like an extraction team. He has seen plenty in the middle east. Most likely private contractors."

"Limited private contractors are operating on US soil." Jacob looked confused.

The chime of the little bell over the door alerting to

the entry of a customer sounded, and the three came forward.

"We give a discount to first responders," Marta called out as she led the trio out of the small office. Her offer came with her straining to speak understandable English. There were four people dressed in city police uniforms standing facing the counter. As a trained agent, she knew there was something wrong. Live through this encounter, Marta thought. Don't break the cover. Marta began to assess. They were not just standing randomly. They were covering the room. Some sort of tactical formation. The look on their faces was focused; they were ready for a rough encounter. And even though their uniforms and badges said ST. Louis City Police, they were carrying the wrong type of weapons.

"We did not come to get our clothes pressed. We had a few questions." The tall, strong-looking man in his forties spoke. He had a pockmarked face and a steely gaze like he was reading a map that was sitting too far away.

There were two other male officers and two female officers in the cleaners. An additional male officer could be seen through the storefront window guarding the entrance to the cleaners. A stocky pale-skinned female officer with a red buzz cut started to walk behind the counter, and Moses blocked her.

"Step aside, Sambo," Red commanded.

Mosses stood there staring straight ahead and not moving. He had endured many racial insults in the military academy and knew them for what they were.

"Relax, Mosses, we have nothing to hide," Jacob called to Mosses.

"That's right Nigger Jim, be a good nigger and step aside, and while you are at it, show me some ID. And it had better not be your grandmother's food stamp card."

"It is not necessary to insult him," Jacob shouted from the back of the room.

"I tell you what, why do you all pony up some current valid ID." The officer in charge commanded.

Red and Mosses still seemed locked in, staring at each other. Red made a half turn to fake, then spun around to punch Mosses in the face.

Mosses had boxed golden gloves before being accepted at West Point. Mosses slipped her punch and let the force from the would-be blow cause her to fall off balance and almost hit the floor. The other officers found this entertaining. Red did not. Red raced toward Mosses to grab him and wrestle him, but he held up the heel of his hand, and it hit her like the force of running full speed into a wall. She dropped to her knees.

"Stop this shit. The kid is clearly not trained to stand still and take a beating. No peaceful protesting or singing we shall overcome while you beat the shit out of him." The commander praised the skill level of Mosses. Moses leaned forward to help the female officer up; the universal no harm intended move. She lay half kneeling and nursing a nosebleed. Then something Mosses had never before experienced overtook him. The light in the room seemed to dim, and a rush of air seemed to pass his ears. For a moment, he could swear he heard the voice of his late grandmother singing one of the old negro spirituals she used to sign on her way to church in Georgia. Mosses looked over at Marta and could not identify the look on her face, but she was staring at him. His midsection to be more precise. It hurt. He looked down at his midsection, and there was Red's hand. She had something in it. It was the handle of a knife, and the blade was buried deep within his stomach.

Mosses was sad not that he knew he was dying but that he had let Marta and Jacob down. He was the youngest of the team, and his inexperience was marring the operation. There was screaming from behind him. Then the screaming stopped at the end of automatic gunfire. It was Jacob that had been silenced.

"Bag the bodies if there is a bounty on either of them, I want us to get it. Bag the chick." The commander ordered. "And call the translator team that was recommended let's see what this one has to say."

Marta felt the nylon tie bind her from the back as a dark see through hood was placed over her head. She felt an over personal and over aggressive searching of her person and one last statement rang in her ears. It was from the commander. "Alright boys and girls let's get the fuck out of her before the real cops show up."

"SO. THIS IS THE PART where I fold the whipped egg whites into the batter." Alexis stated to Vincent Garrison. Vincent felt proud that his daughter Lisa and his next-door neighbor's daughter Alexis love to get cooking lessons from him. He also tutored them both in math even though Lisa, being eighteen and preparing for college, was at a higher level than Alexis.

"Now the trick is to wait until the oil is just the right temperature before adding the batter. Corn oil works best for pancakes and canola if you don't have it but never use a meat rendering.

The smoke point is too low. It will burn your product and taste burned."

"Oh my God what are you doing." Lowell Waterman entered the room from the kitchen. The Waterman's are Vincent Garrisons neighbors. The Garrison back door has a keypad lock and Vincent insisted that all the Waterman's know the combination. Lowell entered with his nine-year-old son Donny.

"Cornflakes," Donny screamed, and the small copper-colored puppy named Cornflakes rushed out to greet his favorite playmate.

"Mr. Garrison is teaching me to make Mississippi Pecan Pancakes."

"Not that. Where is your robe?" Lowell scolded.

"Well, I was cooking, and it was warm. Besides, Mr. Garrison doesn't see me that way." She turned to Vincent. "Do you." Alexis stood wearing a nightshirt that was probably the perfect size two years ago but now looked like she was blossoming in all the right places.

Vincent walked over to where Alexis had left the robe and handed it to her. "It is not about how I look at you. It is about your father asking you to do something and you questioning it. Do what he asks first. Then ask your question. The time we fathers have with our daughters goes so fast it need not be marred with defiance."

"God, I am sorry, Daddy. Sit, and you can be my first customer."

Lowell shot Vincent a look of gratitude for the parental backup.

"Oh my," Lowell exclaimed as he tasted the pancakes. "Why aren't you teaching my wife to cook."

"Because she is hopeless," Alexis mumbled.

"I heard that." Sharon Waterman explained, appearing from the kitchen in search of her missing family. "You are a traitor, Lowell Waterman. I send you to retrieve my children, and I find you eating pancakes."

"It was my duty as a parent to check her culinary progress.

And my God, are there good."

"Sit mom, you get the next batch."

"Mr. Garrison, Cornflakes says he wants to go outside to do his business," Donny called over the other conversation.

"Then, by all means take him outside, and maybe someday you can let me in on how the two of you talk to each other. It could save me countless carpet cleanings."

This brought a round of laughs from the group.

"Will Lisa be back soon?" Susan Waterman asked Vincent with a note of concern ringing in her voice.

"She is visiting her mom in Chicago. She should be back tomorrow. I keep thinking she will be off to college soon, and my nest will be empty." Vincent may have started the statement to be glib, but his eyes gave him away.

Also by Alex Mitchell